CUMBRIA LIBRARIES
3 8003 04754 3533

KT-491-497
County Council
Libraries, books and more...........

Please return/renew this item by the last date shown.
Library items may also be renewed by phone on
030 33 33 1234 (24hours) or via our website

www.cumbria.gov.uk/libraries

Cumbria Libraries
CLIC
Interactive Catalogue

Ask for a CLIC password

To everyone who plays fair!

ORCHARD BOOKS

First published in Great Britain in 2016 by The Watts Publishing Group

1 3 5 7 9 10 8 6 4 2

© 2016 Rainbow Magic Limited.
© 2016 HIT Entertainment Limited.
Illustrations © Orchard Books 2016

The moral rights of the author and illustrator have been asserted.
All characters and events in this publication, other than those clearly in the public domain, are fictitious and any resemblance to real persons, living or dead, is purely coincidental.

All rights reserved.
No part of this publication may be reproduced, stored in a retrieval system, or transmitted, in any form or by any means, without the prior permission in writing of the publisher, nor be otherwise circulated in any form of binding or cover other than that in which it is published and without a similar condition including this condition being imposed on the subsequent purchaser.

A CIP catalogue record for this book is available from the British Library.

ISBN 978 1 40834 164 3

Printed and bound in Great Britain by CPI Group (UK) Ltd, Croydon, CR0 4YY

The paper and board used in this book are made from wood from responsible sources

Orchard Books
An imprint of Hachette Children's Group
Part of The Watts Publishing Group Limited
Carmelite House, 50 Victoria Embankment, London EC4Y 0DZ

An Hachette UK Company
www.hachette.co.uk
www.hachettechildrens.co.uk

Melissa the Sports Fairy

by Daisy Meadows

www.rainbowmagic.co.uk

The Fairyland Palace

Fairyland

Mermaid Lake

Swimming Pool

Trampolines

Volleyball

Rainspell Beach

Jack Frost's
Ice Castle
Mermaid
Cottage
Dolphin
Cottage
Rainspell
Island

Jack Frost's Spell

Melissa says if you join in,
It doesn't matter if you win.
What rubbish! In this competition,
Winning is my one ambition.

I'm not wasting time on training.
Hard work makes me start complaining.
I'll steal her things so I can cheat,
And laugh at all the fools I beat!

The Magical
Gold Medal

Contents

Return to Rainspell

"What are you thinking about?" Rachel Walker asked her best friend, Kirsty Tate.

Kirsty was leaning over the railings of the boat that was taking them to Rainspell Island. She was gazing down at the blue-green waves and her hair was blowing in the breeze.

"I was thinking about the day we met on this boat," said Kirsty, turning to look at Rachel. "It was one of the best days ever. I found a wonderful best friend – and I met real fairies too."

Rachel smiled back at her. Together, they had met many fairies since then, and had many magical adventures. Now they were returning to the island for the exciting Rainspell Games.

"I'm so glad that our parents agreed to bring us here for the Games," said Rachel. "We'll even be staying in Mermaid Cottage and Dolphin Cottage, just like when we met the Rainbow Fairies. It's perfect."

It was the start of the summer holidays, and the girls were looking forward to spending lots of time together. They

could hardly wait to explore the island's green fields and sandy beaches again.

"I hope we see some fairies too," Kirsty added. "It always feels as if there's magic in the air when we're here."

When the ferry docked, Rachel and Kirsty were the first passengers to step onto the island. They gazed across to the other side of the harbour, where their cottages stood on a golden beach.

"We'll get taxis to take us to the cottages," said Mr Walker. "We seem to have brought more bags with us this time!"

While their parents went to find the taxis, Rachel and Kirsty drew in deep breaths of the fresh sea air and listened to the sound of the waves splashing against the harbour wall.

"I'm going to have the same bedroom as before," said Rachel, thinking of the little attic room she had loved so much. "Isn't it wonderful to be back again?"

Kirsty nodded, looking at a group of people on the beach. They were all wearing rainbow-coloured caps and jackets with 'Rainspell Games' written on the back.

"They must be the competitors," said Kirsty.

There was a crowd of people taking photographs of them and calling out good luck wishes. There were also some people wearing rainbow-coloured bibs.

"I think they're the stewards," said Rachel. "They'll help to organise the Games, and make sure that everything goes smoothly."

"Some of them don't seem very interested in the competitors," said Kirsty.

Three of the stewards were standing in a huddle, a short distance away from the others. They were bending over something that they were holding between them, and taking no notice of the happy crowd nearby.

Just then, Rachel noticed a big placard beside them.

RAINSPELL ISLAND GAMES SCHEDULE

The Games will begin promptly at midday.

The challenges are:

1. Beach volleyball

2. Trampolining

3. Diving

There will be no break between events 2 and 3. The fitness and stamina of the competitors will be tested to their limits.

We wish all competitors the best of luck!

"Goodness, it sounds really hard," said Kirsty. "They must have trained for months to be fit enough."

"I can't wait to watch them," Rachel added. "I wonder if they're nervous."

The girls looked over at the competitors again.

"I think they look excited," said Kirsty.

Just then, Kirsty's dad called them over.

"We've found two taxis, girls," he said. "Come on – it's time to go to our cottages!"

An Extra Passenger

The Tates got into the first taxi and the Walkers took the second. As they were driving along the little beach road to the cottage, Kirsty turned around in the back of the car and waved. Rachel waved back, and then she noticed something strange. The light on top of the taxi was shining very brightly.

"That's odd," she said to herself. "The light shouldn't be on when the taxi has passengers in it."

As she watched, the light started to glow even more brightly, until it was sparkling with light. Then a tiny, smiling face peeped around the light, winked at Rachel and disappeared again. Rachel rubbed her eyes.

"I wish Kirsty was here," she said under her breath. "Did I really see that?"

She looked again, but the taxi light was off and there was no fairy in sight.

"I hope I didn't imagine it," Rachel murmured to herself. "I'm so excited to

be back here, I keep expecting to see fairies everywhere!"

Mrs Walker gave her a curious look. "What are you muttering about, love?" she asked.

"I was just thinking about how exciting it is to be back on Rainspell Island," said Rachel. "Oh, look – we're here!"

The taxi stopped outside the pretty cottages where they had stayed before. Rachel jumped out of the car and hurried over to Kirsty's taxi. She walked all around it, looking up at the light, but there was definitely no fairy to be seen. Kirsty stared at her in surprise. She knew at once that something strange had happened. Rachel was longing to talk to Kirsty about it, but her parents were waiting for her.

"Let's go and unpack," said Mr Walker. "Come on, Rachel."

"Please could we help each other unpack?" Rachel asked. "We've got so much to talk about!"

The Walkers and the Tates laughed.

"You two never stop talking and sharing secrets," said Mr Walker, smiling. "But the answer is yes, as long as it's OK with Kirsty's parents?"

Mr and Mrs Tate agreed, and the girls hurried into Dolphin Cottage. They wheeled Kirsty's suitcase into her bedroom and shut the door. At once, Kirsty turned to face her.

"Well?" she asked, her eyes sparkling. "What's happened?"

"I think I saw a fairy on top of your taxi," said Rachel, her words tumbling out in her excitement.

Kirsty clapped her hands together and jumped up and down a few times.

"I knew we'd have fairy adventures as soon as we arrived!" she said, grinning. "Who was it? Ruby the Red Fairy?"

Ruby had a very special place in their hearts, because she had been the first fairy they had ever met. Rachel shook her head.

"It wasn't Ruby," she said. "I don't think we've ever met her before – I didn't recognise her. I only really glimpsed her for a second."

Kirsty bit her lip.

"You don't think you could have imagined her, do you?" she asked.

"I wasn't seeing things," said Rachel, but she was beginning to feel doubtful. "At least … I hope I wasn't!"

"You weren't," said a tinkling voice. "What you saw was real, Rachel!"

With a whooshing sound, a tiny fairy darted out from under the luggage label of Kirsty's suitcase.

"You're the fairy I saw on the taxi!" Rachel exclaimed. "It's wonderful to meet you!"

Thieves on the Island

"I'm Melissa the Sports Fairy," said their surprise visitor.

She was wearing a green tracksuit with purple trainers, and her dark hair was styled in a long, swinging plait.

"It's great to meet you, Melissa," said Kirsty. "Are you on the island for the Games, like us?"

"Yes," said Melissa. "I've been looking forward to it for ages, but that's not why I came to find you."

"What do you mean?" Rachel asked.

Melissa sighed and fluttered over to Kirsty's bed, where she sat down and crossed her legs.

"I was really pleased when I saw you arrive on the boat," she explained. "You see, something awful has just happened. My most precious belongings have been stolen, and I don't know what to do."

"Oh, Melissa, you poor thing," said Kirsty, sitting down beside her. "Will you

tell us about it?"

"I brought my magical gold medal, my daring dumbbells and my sparkling stopwatch to the island," said Melissa. "I knew that they would make sure that the Games go smoothly. I hid them in the announcer's tent, but while I was watching the competitors on the beach, someone crept into the tent and stole them!"

"Oh, no," said Rachel. "Does that mean that the Rainspell Games will go wrong today?"

"I'm afraid so," said Melissa. "And not just the Rainspell Games. I'm supposed to take my objects back home for the Fairyland Games later this afternoon. Without them, both the competitions will be ruined."

"Do you have any idea who might have taken them?" Kirsty asked.

Melissa nodded. "I searched for clues as soon as I realised they'd been stolen," she said. "There were big, clumpy prints in the soil outside the tent."

"Jack Frost and his goblins," said Rachel at once.

"Yes, I think so," said Melissa. "He hasn't caused much trouble in Fairyland lately – we should have guessed he was plotting something! Will you two help me to get my magical objects back before the Games are ruined?"

"Of course," Kirsty replied.

"We just have to unpack first," said Rachel. "We promised our parents that we would."

Melissa winked at her and then waved

her wand in the air. Instantly, Kirsty's suitcase unzipped itself and opened. Neatly folded clothes whizzed through the air as drawers and wardrobe doors opened to let them in. It only took a few seconds before the suitcase was empty and the room was tidy.

"You'll find that your suitcase is unpacked too, Rachel," said Melissa. "Now you are free to come with me!"

With Melissa hidden safely in Rachel's tunic pocket, the girls hurried to ask for permission to go down to the beach.

"Goodness, that was quick!" said Mrs Walker in surprise. "Are all your things unpacked?"

"Yes," said Rachel, with a grin. "It didn't take as long as we expected."

"All right, girls, off you go," Mrs Walker agreed. "I've still got lots to unpack, but we'll see you at midday when the Games begin."

The girls hurried to the beach and saw that the crowds were still there. A microphone had been set up, and some official-looking people were standing beside it.

"It looks as if the opening speeches are about to begin," said Kirsty.

Most of the stewards were bustling around, busily trying to get everything ready. But the three stewards who the girls had noticed earlier were not working. They were shuffling away from the crowd as if they wanted to escape.

"Those stewards really are very odd," said Rachel.

Suddenly, Kirsty gasped and clutched Rachel's arm.

"Look at their enormous feet!" she exclaimed. "They're not stewards at all. They're goblins!"

A Late Arrival

Melissa poked her head out of Rachel's pocket.

"Follow them!" she whispered, in an urgent voice. "They might have my magical objects!"

The goblins left the beach and disappeared around the corner of a big beach hut. Rachel and Kirsty hurried after them, and then darted backwards.

The goblins hadn't gone far – they were waiting just around the corner. Luckily they hadn't noticed the girls. They were too busy tussling with each other over something they were all trying to hold.

"Did you see what was in their hands?" Kirsty asked.

Rachel shook her head. "We need to get another look," she said.

Just then, they heard the piercing whine of a microphone. The speeches were beginning. The chief organiser stepped onto a small podium and introduced himself.

"My name is Leo Read," he said. "Welcome to Rainspell Island Games! We hope you'll have a great time today. There are lots of competitors hoping to be named the winner, and I'm sure you'll

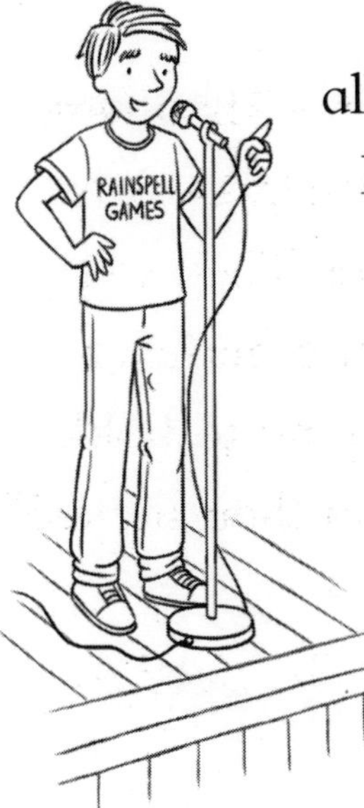

all enjoy cheering them on. But just remember that it's the winning that counts, not the taking part. And a little bit of cheating – well – it's all part of the fun, isn't it?"

Rachel and Kirsty exchanged horrified glances, but no one else seemed to have noticed that anything was wrong. Then they heard the explosive sound of goblin giggles. They peered around the corner again, and this time they saw a flash of gold in the goblins' hands. Melissa let out a little squeak and then clapped her hand over her mouth. She fluttered up to hover between the two girls.

"That's my gold medal!" she whispered. "It's one of my magical objects!"

"What does it do?" Rachel asked.

"It helps the best person win," said Melissa. "Without it, races and sporting competitions won't be fair. The people who deserve to win – the ones who have worked and trained really hard – will lose to the cheats and the tricksters. And no one will do anything to stop it from happening!"

"*We* will," said Kirsty in a firm voice.

"As soon as we can, we'll get your gold medal back. Let's find a place to sit from where we can watch the goblins and wait for our chance."

Melissa tucked herself back into Rachel's pocket, and the girls chose a good place on the beach. They settled down as the competitors lined up beside ten volleyball nets.

"We have twenty brave competitors today, folks," Leo Read was saying. "No … wait … twenty-one. A last-minute competitor has joined us. Now, the first stage is the beach volleyball competition. This will be followed by the trampolining challenge. As soon as each competitor has reached the required height, they will move straight on to the final stage – the diving contest."

Just then, the competitors shuffled along to make room for the last-minute entry. Leo Read kept talking, but the girls didn't hear another word. The twenty-first competitor was Jack Frost!

He was wearing a pair of sparkling blue shorts and a white T-shirt with a blue snowflake on it. Leo Read was walking along the line now, introducing each person. When he reached Jack Frost, Rachel winced and Kirsty buried her face in her hands. What on earth was he going to say?

"Tell us your name and a little bit about yourself," said Leo Read, holding the microphone up to Jack Frost's mouth.

"They call me 'The Frost'," said Jack Frost with a horrid grin. "And I'm going to do whatever it takes to win today."

"That's why he stole your objects, Melissa," Rachel whispered. "He wants to be a winner. That's all he cares about."

She looked at the goblins. They were nudging each other and laughing.

"Remember the rules, everyone," said Leo Read, speaking to the competitors.

"The only things you can use in this game are your hands. Nothing else is allowed. Good luck to each and every one of you. Let the Games begin!"

Beach Cheats

The whistle blew, and the ten games of volleyball began. Jack Frost had joined a team of two.

"He doesn't even know how to play this game," said Melissa with a groan.

"I think he's got the idea," said Kirsty in astonishment. "Look – he's jumping higher than all the others, and he's hitting the ball more often than anyone."

"But he's cheating!" cried Rachel, who had turned back from watching the goblins. "Look – he's got a big foam hand over his own to make sure he can hit the ball."

Either the Games organisers hadn't noticed or they didn't care. The watching crowds had noticed, but they didn't seem to mind at all.

"Ha ha, what a brilliant cheat!" shouted one man nearby.

"The Frost is a genius!" yelled another. "Well done!"

"No one can beat The Frost!" squawked the goblins.

They were dancing around in glee as Jack Frost continued to do well. In frustration, some of the other competitors were starting to cheat too. The stewards had noticed this and were moving forwards, frowning. Melissa chewed her fingernails with worry.

"Soon no one will be sticking to the rules," she said. "We have to do something!"

Rachel jumped to her feet. "We can't wait for the goblins to take their eyes off the medal," she said to Kirsty. "If we don't do something quickly, all the competitors will be disqualified and the Games will be spoiled. I'll distract the goblins and you try to grab the medal. Come on!"

They hurried back towards the goblins, and then Rachel flipped herself forwards onto her hands and started to cartwheel around.

Melissa clung on to Rachel's pocket as tightly as she could.

"This is brilliant!" she cried.

The goblins were watching Rachel in astonishment, and Kirsty knew that this was her chance. She tiptoed up behind the one who had the medal in his hand but, just as she reached him, he put the medal around his neck. Rachel stopped doing cartwheels and tried to catch her breath.

"That was the best ride ever," said Melissa from inside Rachel's pocket. "I'm so dizzy!"

For a moment, Kirsty wondered whether to just beg the goblins to give her the medal. Then she had a better idea. She laughed and put her arm around Rachel.

"My friend does the best cartwheels I've ever seen," she said. "I bet you can't do cartwheels as well as she can."

"Oh, yeah?" said the goblins all together. "Watch this!"

They started to cartwheel around the girls, kicking their legs up and bumping into each other. The girls only had to wait a few seconds before the medal dropped from the goblin's neck and fell onto the ground.

"Quick, Melissa!" Rachel whispered.

Melissa zoomed out of Rachel's pocket and seized the medal with both hands. As soon as she touched it, it shrank to fairy size. She put it around her neck and spun around in delight.

"My gold medal is back where it belongs!" she said happily. "Thank you, girls! You've been so kind – and so clever!"

The goblins were now lying flat on their backs, complaining that they felt dizzy. Grinning, the girls and Melissa turned back to watch the end of the volleyball game.

"Jack Frost's team has already won – look," said Kirsty, pointing to where Jack Frost was standing with his chest puffed out proudly. "We were too late."

"No, we weren't," said Melissa. "Listen

to the crowd."

No one was praising cheaters now. All the shouts were to praise competitors for being good sports. The girls watched as the last two teams battled it out on the sand. The ball flew through the air between them, and then one of the competitors shook his head.

"I'm sorry," he called out. "I just used an open hand to hit the ball, and that's against the rules."

"Well done for being honest!" boomed Leo Read through the microphone.

"That's it, folks! The volleyball is over and we have our winners. The trampolining challenge will begin immediately. Follow me!"

Rachel, Kirsty and Melissa shared happy smiles.

"We did it!" said Melissa. "We make a pretty good team too, don't we?"

They laughed, but then Kirsty's smile faded a little.

"The Rainspell Games and the Fairyland Games are still in danger," she said. "I hope that we can get the other

magical objects back before the Games are ruined."

"Of course we can," said Melissa, patting her on the shoulder. "I'm starting to see that with you to help me, anything is possible!"

The Daring Dumbbells

Contents

Green Cheerleaders

Rachel and Kirsty followed the chief organiser Leo Read, the competitors and the spectators to the top of the beach, where the trampolines were set up. Melissa had tucked herself back into Rachel's pocket, her gold medal safely around her neck again.

"The competitors look nervous," said Kirsty. "All except Jack Frost."

The Ice Lord, who had been busy ordering everyone to call him 'The Frost', was now strutting around, bumping other competitors out of his way. As the girls watched, he elbowed a burly man in the arm. The man's lips trembled, his chin wobbled, and then he burst into floods of tears.

"Goodness me!" said Rachel. "Jack Frost shouldn't be pushing people, but I can't believe it hurt that much. I thought the competitors were supposed to be strong and fit and tough."

"I don't think they are," said Kirsty. "I've just seen another one in tears over there because she slightly grazed her knee."

Melissa peeped up at them from her hiding place.

"Usually they *are* all the things you said," she whispered. "They're only behaving so feebly because Jack Frost and his goblins have my daring dumbbells."

"What do they do?" asked Rachel.

"They help competitors and sportspeople to feel fit and strong," said Melissa. "While they're missing, I'm afraid the competitors will not be on good enough form to complete the event. They'll cry every time they fall over and need first aid for every tiny scrape and bump. The Games will be ruined!"

"All this trouble, just because Jack Frost wants to be a winner," said Kirsty, feeling cross. "It's not fair."

"That's never stopped him before," Rachel pointed out.

Just then, the three goblins stomped up to join the crowd, still looking a little dizzy from all the cartwheels. They shot bad-tempered looks at the girls.

"You stole our medal," one of them snapped at Rachel.

"Nonsense," said Rachel. "We returned it to its rightful owner."

"Humph," said the goblin, turning away.

He and the other goblins were now wearing T-shirts with 'THE FROST – WINNER!' written on them in sparkling blue sequins. Ignoring the girls, they started doing star jumps, and then suddenly they burst into a little song-and-dance routine. People scattered as the goblins kicked their legs and flung out their arms.

"Frost! Frost! He's our guy!
He can jump and touch the sky!
Frost! Frost! He's the best!
Stick his photo on your vest!"

"Oh, dear," Kirsty groaned. "What on earth are they going to say next?"

"I think we're about to find out," said Rachel.

The goblins were now balancing on each other's shoulders, waving flags of Jack Frost's face.

"Frost! Frost! He's no fool!

He makes spiky beards look cool!

Frost! Frost! Take a bow!

All the rest should give up now!"

Suddenly, Kirsty gasped. The goblin at the bottom of the pile was not holding flags like the other two. Instead, there were two purple weights in his hands.

"Melissa, look!" Kirsty said in an urgent whisper. "Are those your daring dumbbells?"

Melissa poked her head out of Rachel's pocket and let out an excited squeak.

"Yes, they're mine," she said, biting her lip. "Oh, dear, I can't bear to see them in the hands of those naughty goblins."

"We're going to get them back," said Rachel, feeling determined. "We just have to work out *how*!"

Flying Over Rainspell

Kirsty marched towards the goblins, but she was only halfway there when they spotted her coming.

"Scatter!" shouted the goblin holding the dumbbells.

The three goblins dived into the growing crowd and vanished from sight.

"We have to follow them!" Kirsty exclaimed.

"Let me turn you into fairies," said Melissa. "It'll be easier to look for the goblins if you can fly – and we'll be able to keep an eye on the trampolining too."

Rachel and Kirsty looked around. Everyone in the crowd was looking at the competitors as they lined up beside the trampolines.

"Come on," said Rachel. "Let's go behind the beach hut where the goblins hid earlier. No one's looking."

They raced down to the beach hut and slipped out of sight. No one could see them – and there weren't even any boats out at sea. Melissa flew out of Rachel's pocket and waved her tiny wand. Little purple sparkles spiralled from her wand

tip and wound
around Rachel
and Kirsty.
They felt
a rush of
excitement
as they
shrank to
fairy size
and their wings
lifted them into the
air.

"Follow me!" Melissa cried, zooming back towards the crowd. "We have to find that goblin!"

Flying high above the beach, the three fairies scanned the crowd, but it was impossible to see the goblin among all the people.

"I can see Mum and Dad," said Kirsty, peering down. "Your parents are with them too, Rachel. I wish we could wave to them!"

A microphone whined and the girls saw Leo Read step up to a podium.

"We are about to begin the second section of the Rainspell Games," he announced. "Each competitor must bounce to the required height before they can leave the trampolines and start the third and final section – the diving."

He paused for the crowd to cheer and applaud. Most of the competitors were

looking serious and scared. Jack Frost, however, was doing a few last-minute squats and flexing his arm muscles.

"Please remember the rules," Leo Read went on, turning to face the competitors. "Shorts and tops must stay on while you are on the trampolines, and only be removed when you are ready to dive. As soon as you have bounced to the correct height, leave the trampolines, pull off your shorts and top and head over to the pool for the diving event. All right, take your positions!"

As the competitors stepped up to the trampolines, Jack Frost pulled off his shorts and top. Underneath, he was wearing an old-fashioned swimsuit with blue-and-white stripes.

"He's not allowed to do that yet," Melissa said with a groan. "He's breaking the rules."

One of the stewards stepped forward and opened her mouth to say something, but Jack Frost glared at her and she stepped back again.

"Competitors!" Leo Read called out. "Ready, steady, BOUNCE!"

Bouncing on the Beach

BOING! BOING! The beach was filled with the twang of trampoline springs and the cheers of spectators. But only one of the competitors was whooping – The Frost! He cackled and squealed as he bounced higher and higher, but the other competitors were making very different noises.

"YOWEEE!"

"OOOH!"

"ARGH!"

They had only bounced three or four times, but some of the competitors were already staggering away from the trampolines.

"I'm too tired!" wailed one.

"My legs ache!" cried another.

One of the competitors lost her balance and tumbled off her trampoline. She grazed her knee and started to sob.

The three fairies were hovering above, and Melissa sighed and shook her head.

"This is ridiculous," said Rachel. "Soon there will be no competitors left!"

Kirsty corrected her. "There will be *one* left."

Jack Frost was bouncing higher than all the other competitors, grinning as he flew into the air. He hooted with laughter, lifting his knees like a frog, kicking them like scissors and even doing the splits in mid-air.

There was a steward standing next to each trampoline, holding a pole upright.

"As soon as the competitors have jumped higher than the pole, they can move on to the diving section," said Rachel. "It looks as if Jack Frost will reach it soon. He's jumping the highest."

"As long as he or the goblins have the dumbbells, he will feel fit and strong," said Melissa. "He'll be able to keep going, no matter how uncomfortable he is."

Rachel and Kirsty kept looking around for a glimpse of the goblins, but they were not in sight. Then they heard a shriek of triumph and a cheer from the crowd.

"He's done it," said Kirsty, wringing her hands. "Jack Frost is the first competitor to jump higher than the pole."

They watched as he jumped down and jogged over to the swimming pool.

"Congratulations to The Frost!" said

Leo Read. "He's the first one to reach the final section. He's now entering the diving stage. Competitors have to perform three dives – one straight, one backwards and one including roly-polies. There is an aid station beside the pool offering refreshments, and plasters for any grazed knees."

Jack Frost waved to the spectators as he headed for the steps up to the diving platform.

"No break needed for The Frost," Leo Read continued. "What a competitor!"

"If we don't find those goblins soon, Jack Frost will win the Rainspell Games," said Melissa. "Look at the other competitors."

The three friends looked over at the other athletes. Some had reached the top of the pole, but they were staggering away from the trampolines as if they were almost too tired to walk.

"We have just eleven competitors left," Leo Read boomed through the microphone. "We wish them all the best of luck."

"They're going to need more than luck," said Rachel. "Where *have* those goblins hidden?"

One Daring Diver

The competitors who had dropped out were lying down outside the announcer's tent, fast asleep. Meanwhile, Jack Frost was climbing the ladder to the high diving platform. The board stretched out over a bright blue pool, and it was so high that it almost reached the point where the fairies were hovering. Some of the other competitors were following Jack Frost, pulling pained faces.

"My legs are so wobbly," moaned one man.

"My knees feel as if they might fall off," said another.

"Pathetic," Jack Frost muttered.

"Losers!"

"Those other competitors look as if they belong in the aid station," said Kirsty.

She glanced down at the tent that housed the aid station, and then she clutched at the others.

"What's the matter?" Rachel asked.

"Look who's in charge of aid!" Kirsty exclaimed.

The three goblins from earlier were standing in the entrance of the aid station, staring up at Jack Frost as he walked along the diving board. At once, Melissa zoomed down towards them, followed by Rachel and Kirsty. They swooped under the side of the tent and hid beneath the table.

"I don't want to watch silly humans jumping off a silly board," said one goblin, who had three pimples on the tip of his nose.

"Look!" whispered Rachel. "He's holding the dumbbells!"

The fairies shared excited smiles. They had found them! Now all they had to do was figure out a way to get them back. But the goblin was holding on to them very tightly.

"I want some of that fruit," said the second goblin, pointing over to a large bowl of fruit.

"The fruit is for the competitors, not the goblins," said Melissa in a low voice.

But the goblins didn't care about that. Two of them rushed over to the table and started squabbling over the bowl.

"Give me that peach!"

"It's mine!"

"Let go!"

The fairies heard a squashy, squelchy sound as the goblins splatted each other with ripe peaches.

The pimply goblin shook the dumbbells and scowled at them.

"Stop mucking about, you two," he squawked. "Jack Frost won't like it if you miss his dive."

The fairies peered up at the diving board, and the two squabbling goblins paused their fruit fight as Jack Frost stepped to the very edge. He lifted his arms into an arch shape over his head and rose up on his tiptoes. Then he sprang up and performed a perfect dive, entering the water with barely a splash.

"Thanks to the dumbbells, he has no fear," said Melissa.

"But the others look terrified," said Rachel.

The next diver was trembling on the end of the diving board. As she leaped off, she squealed and panicked, entering the water with a loud belly flop. Behind her, the other competitors were wobbling on the ladder, or refusing to climb it at all.

"The diving event is going to be completely ruined if we can't get the dumbbells back," said Kirsty.

"How can we get them back, though?" asked Melissa. "He'll see us if we come out of our hiding place. It's hopeless!"

"We never give up hope," said Rachel, smiling at the fairy.

"I've got an idea that might work," Kirsty added. "Goblins love getting messy and squabbling, and those two goblins with the peaches have already started. Melissa, could you add lots of food to the table – things that could get the goblins really messy? If the pimply goblin joins in, we might be able to get the dumbbells back while he's distracted."

Delicious Distraction

Melissa raised her wand.

"Jelly, eggs and treacle tarts –
That's how every food fight starts.
Spaghetti, soup and custard pies
Will catch these greedy goblins' eyes!"

Rachel crept out from under the table and took a peek at the top. It was laden

with lots of delicious things to eat. She climbed back under and nodded at Melissa.

"Those things will be very, very messy indeed," she said.

Almost instantly, there were squeals of delight from the goblins as they saw the food. Two of the goblins plunged

their hands in, grabbing whatever they could, shoving some into their faces, and throwing some at each other. But the pimply goblin stayed where he was, holding on to the dumbbells. As the fairies watched, he started hopping from foot to foot.

"He's desperate to join in," Kirsty whispered.

Rachel looked out at the crowd gathering around the pool. All eyes were on the diving – no one was paying attention to the aid station. Jack Frost was climbing the ladder again. Rachel crossed her fingers.

The gobbling, slurping and splatting sounds that the two goblins were making grew louder and louder. The fairies listened to them pushing and shoving each other, and then it sounded as if they were battling over the same thing.

"Mine! I saw it first!"

"No, mine! Hand it over!"

There was a moment of quiet, and then plates and bowls started smashing around them. Trifles went *SPLAT!* beside the table and tiny sweets skittered across the ground like marbles. It was too much for the pimply goblin. He darted forward, shoved the dumbbells under the table and went to join the fun. Melissa, Rachel and Kirsty stared down at the dumbbells in astonishment. They looked at each other for a moment, and then had to put their hands over their mouths to stifle their laughter.

"He handed them straight to us!" Melissa said. "I can't believe it."

She reached out and touched the purple dumbbells. Instantly, they shrank to their usual size, and Melissa picked them up.

"They're back in safe hands," said Rachel, feeling excited. "Now, let's go and see if anything has changed about the diving!"

They zoomed out of the tent, unnoticed by the squabbling goblins, and were almost deafened by the roar of the crowd. Suddenly, the competitors were darting up the ladder and almost flying off the diving board, twisting and turning through the air with skill and ease. Then it was Jack Frost's turn.

"It's the last dive – The Frost!" Leo Read bellowed into the microphone. "What has he got in store for us this time?"

Jack Frost wobbled on the end of the board. The three fairies zoomed upwards and caught his eye as he glanced around.

He scowled when he saw them, and then he spotted the dumbbells in Melissa's hands.

"You interfering fairies!" he roared. "Those idiot goblins!"

Enraged, he shook his fist at the fairies and gave a sudden wobble. Flailing his arms, he completely lost his balance and toppled off the board.

SPLAT!

He did an enormous belly flop into the water. The crowd let out an "Oooh" of sympathy as Jack Frost scrabbled out of the water, dripping wet and furious. He stomped out of sight behind the aid station, and then there was a flash of blue.

"Did you see that?" Kirsty cried. "What has he done?"

They whooshed after him, but when they flew around behind the aid station, there was no one in sight. Jack Frost had vanished.

"He must have gone back to Fairyland," Melissa exclaimed. "Girls, will you come with me and try to find my sparkling stopwatch? I have to follow him, even if it's dangerous. Two sets of Games depend upon me."

"No, they depend upon *us*," said Rachel, putting her arms around the worried fairy. "We're friends, and that means we work as a team."

Melissa smiled. "You two are the best," she said, raising her wand. "OK, Fairyland, here we come!"

The Sparkling Stopwatch

Contents

Rachel and Kirsty were whisked to Fairyland in a swirl of magical sparkles. They arrived on the shores of a vast lake, with Melissa by their side.

"Goodness, that was fast!" said Kirsty, shaking fairy dust from her gauzy wings.

The water was azure blue, and sunlight danced over the ripples. Rachel looked around at the shores of the lake, which were crowded with hundreds of fairies, cheering and waving flags. King Oberon and Queen Titania were sitting on thrones on a raised platform, and enchanted banners fluttered across the

sky saying: 'Welcome to the Fairyland Games'. Beside them was a podium with the numbers one, two and three on it.

"That's where the winner and runners-up will stand," said Melissa above the noise of the crowd. "There are twenty fairies taking part – we've all been looking forward to this day for months!"

The competitors were waiting together at the edge of the lake. Among them the girls recognised several of their friends, including Olympia the Games Fairy and all seven of the Sporty Fairies. Rachel and Kirsty waved to them, and they all waved back. They looked excited and a little bit nervous.

"How are we going to find Jack Frost and get my sparkling stopwatch back?" Melissa exclaimed. "It helps all sporting events to start on time, and the Fairyland Games are supposed to begin any minute now! Without the stopwatch's magic, all the timing will go wrong."

"Let's fly over the crowd again," Rachel suggested. "Jack Frost and his goblins will be easier to spot from above."

They fluttered into the air and zoomed

back and forth over the masses of chattering fairies. They saw lots of their friends, as well as candyfloss stalls, fairground rides and balloon sellers, but they didn't spot a single goblin – or any sign of Jack Frost. Melissa groaned.

"There's no time left," she said. "Everyone is waiting for me to declare the Games open, and I can't make them wait any longer."

"Couldn't you explain what's happened and hold the Games when the stopwatch has been found?" Kirsty asked.

A determined look flashed across Melissa's face.

"I won't allow Jack Frost to spoil a day we've all been looking forward to so much," she said. "He wants to ruin things for the fairies, and I won't let him!"

"Neither will we," said Rachel, darting forwards to give her a hug.

"I just hope that the missing stopwatch doesn't make everything go wrong," Melissa said, her voice wobbling a little.

"We'll help," said Kirsty, squeezing Melissa's hand. "Jack Frost won't win *this* game!"

Rachel and Kirsty stayed hovering above the crowd as Melissa flew down to the podium beside the king and queen. She curtseyed to them and then turned to look at the competitors.

"I am delighted to announce the start of the Fairyland Games!" she called out, and then paused as the crowd of fairies burst into applause. "Welcome to the competitors and the spectators! Today's three events are swimming, spell-work and flying—"

She broke off as a voice called out, "Wait!" and a fairy steward wearing a sparkly mint-green tracksuit darted up to the podium.

"What's wrong?" Melissa asked.

"We're not ready," the steward panted. "The mermaids haven't got the swim course set up yet, and the announcer's tent is still being tidied."

Melissa put her hand to her forehead, and Rachel and Kirsty exchanged a

worried glance. It was obvious that as long as Jack Frost had the sparkling stopwatch, the Fairyland Games would simply fall apart.

"Melissa's busy explaining to the king and queen," said Rachel, peering down. "It's up to us, Kirsty."

"But searching for Jack Frost among this crowd is like looking for a needle in a haystack," Kirsty said. "It seems impossible!"

"Nothing is impossible," said Rachel in a firm voice. "We're in Fairyland! We just have to *think*, Kirsty! Where could Jack Frost be hiding?"

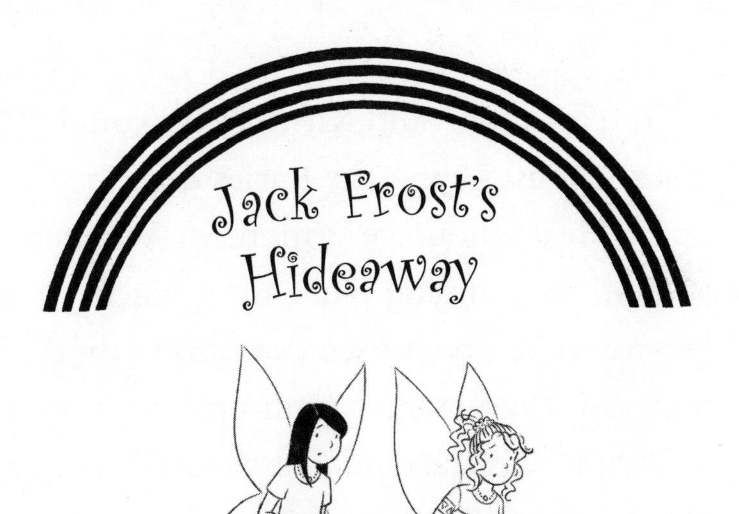

Jack Frost's Hideaway

The girls thought hard as they watched Melissa fly over to help get everything ready.

"If I were Jack Frost," said Rachel, "I'd want to see all these problems I'd created. He is trying to spoil the fun, so I'm sure he'll be watching from somewhere."

"You're right," said Kirsty. "He wouldn't want to miss seeing the fairies getting upset. He'd enjoy every moment. We have to think of a hiding place from where he would be able to see everything that happens – somewhere high up."

They looked around, but the highest place was the platform where the king and queen were sitting.

"He's definitely not there," said Rachel. "And he can't be on the podium because there's nowhere to hide."

Kirsty just shook her head. She couldn't think of where the Ice Lord might be hiding, although she felt sure he was nearby. Just then, a whistle blew and the twenty fairy competitors dived into the water.

"Who blew that whistle?" cried Melissa,

zooming up and looking all around. "Come back, competitors! The course isn't ready yet!"

She and the fairy stewards were flying to and fro, sometimes bumping into each other. The competitors swam back to the shore and crawled out of the water, their wings bedraggled.

"This is turning into a disaster," said Kirsty, looking up as a shadow fell over them. "Even the weather is bad – look at that huge, grey cloud right above us. If I didn't know better, I'd say it was about to snow."

"Oh, *yes*!" Rachel said with a squeak of excitement. "Kirsty, you're a genius!"

"Am I?" Kirsty exclaimed. "What did I do?"

"You made me see what's staring us in the face," Rachel said. "It's just like we said earlier – the best place to see what's going on is from above. Jack Frost is on that cloud!"

"Of course," said Kirsty with a gasp. "He can control snow clouds! Why else would it look like snow in the middle of summer?"

They zoomed upwards side by side until they were hovering just below the cloud. They fluttered a little higher and peered over the edge of the cloud. Jack Frost was sitting cross-legged, holding a stopwatch in one hand and a sandwich in the other.

"That must be the sparkling stopwatch!" Kirsty said in a whisper. "How are we going to get it away from him?"

"I have no idea," Rachel replied, biting her lip. "But I know we'll think of something. Melissa is depending on us."

Jack Frost chuckled as he watched the shambles that was happening below. Melissa was handing out towels to the competitors and trying to prepare them for the real start of the Games. At last they were all in position again.

"Spell-work will follow on immediately from the swimming stage," said Melissa, "so make sure that you come out of the lake with your wands at the ready. Good luck, everyone!"

The real whistle blew, the fairies dived into the lake and the first stage began. The cheers and shouts of encouragement were deafening, but the girls could see that not all the competitors were doing their best swimming. A couple of them had already had to be rescued.

As if he were watching a hilarious show, Jack Frost smiled, took a big bite from his sandwich and glanced around. Then his eyes fell on Rachel and Kirsty. He gave a surprised splutter and spat out his sandwich.

"What are *you* annoying pair doing here?" he snarled, jabbing his bony finger at them and pulling a rude face. "Clear off!"

"We're not going anywhere until you return the stopwatch to its rightful owner," said Rachel.

"I *am* its rightful owner," said Jack Frost, holding up the stopwatch by its chain and dangling it to and fro. "Finders keepers."

"You didn't *find* it; you *stole* it," said Kirsty, feeling outraged.

"Stealers keepers, then," said Jack Frost, sticking out his tongue at her. "It's mine, and I'm keeping it."

"We won't let you," said Rachel, trying to sound brave even though her legs were trembling.

"I'm not as daft as the goblins," said Jack Frost, with an unpleasant grin. "You won't be able to trick me. Give up and go home, and let me enjoy my triumph over the fairies in peace!"

Bedazzled!

"Like Rachel said, we're not going anywhere," said Kirsty.

She sat down on the cloud, and Rachel sat beside her. Jack Frost scowled at them, but he didn't want to miss any more of the chaos he had created. Below, the swimming stage was nearly at an end.

One by one, the fairies waded out of the water and held up their wands. Some of them had gone the wrong way, and still had waterweeds clinging to their wings. Jack Frost laughed so hard that he had to hold on to his belly.

"Those stupid fairies!" he chortled. "Serves them right for trying to have fun!"

"Why do you have to be so mean?" Rachel asked him. "You'd have much

more fun if you joined in."

"Don't talk gobbledygook," said Jack Frost, with a curl of his lip. "Watching the fairies suffer is much more fun than anything else I can imagine!"

He blew a loud raspberry at her and then looked down again. Just then, Rachel and Kirsty heard Melissa's voice announcing the next stage through the microphone.

"Your spell-work challenge is to create a fountain of fairy dust," she told the competitors. "It must shoot as high into the air as possible, and it must contain at least three different colours. The highest fountain will be the winner. Good luck!"

The competitors stood in a row and held their wands above their heads, preparing their best spells.

"It must be very hard not to get distracted by the other spells around you," said Rachel, leaning over the edge of the cloud to watch.

The first fairy-dust fountains began to erupt, but none of them went upwards! Some shot sideways into the crowd, transforming spectators' outfits into every

colour of the rainbow. Others came out of the wrong end of the wand, hitting the ground and changing the colour of the grass. Fairy dust went everywhere, except upwards. Melissa flew back and forth, trying to get their spells under control. Up on the cloud, Jack Frost was beside himself with laughter.

"Hee hee hee! Ha ha ha! Ho ho ho!" He wiped tears from his eyes. "This is the best fun *ever*! I don't know when I've been so entertained! Ha ha ha! I'm laughing so much that I'm crying! I can hardly see what's going on!"

An idea flashed into Kirsty's mind like a firework exploding.

"That's *it*!" she whispered into Rachel's ear. "We have to dazzle Jack Frost so that he can't see us take the stopwatch!"

"That's a wonderful idea," Rachel said

with a grin. "And I know exactly what to dazzle him with!"

Together, they swooped down to the spell-work competition. The ground was thick with fairy dust in every colour imaginable, and the girls scooped up as much of it as they could carry.

"It's like having our arms full of rainbows," said Kirsty, as they flew upwards again.

The girls fluttered up behind Jack Frost. He was still looking down at the fairy competitors, and the girls didn't make a sound as they landed on the soft, fluffy cloud. They tiptoed forwards until they were close behind him, and then Rachel tapped him on the shoulder. When he whirled around, the girls blew every scrap of fairy dust in his face.

"Argh!" Jack Frost roared, waving his arms around to try to flap the fairy dust away. "Stop it! Nasty, cheerful colours! Horrible sparkly fairy dust! Get it off me! Yuck!"

But the fairy dust whirled and spun around him. It was in his mouth, clinging to his eyelashes and coating his beard. The harder he tried to brush it away, the more it attached itself to him. He was

starting to get dizzy. His arms flailed about wildly and then, just as the girls had hoped, he lost his grip on the things he was holding. His sandwich flew up and was caught by a hungry bird, and the sparkling stopwatch twirled through the air and disappeared over the edge of the cloud!

A Magical Competition

"Quickly!" Kirsty cried.

She and Rachel dived after the stopwatch. Jack Frost pulled out his wand and sent thunderbolts crackling into the air around him. Wiping fairy dust from his eyes, he made his cloud swoosh downwards and came face to face with

Rachel and Kirsty. They hovered in front of him with their arms folded.

"How dare you blow fairy dust at me?" Jack Frost screeched.

"Fairy dust can't do you any harm," said Rachel. "We *love* being dazzled by it."

"Where is that stopwatch?" he growled.

With a smile, Rachel unfolded her arms and held up the sparkling stopwatch.

Jack Frost bared his teeth.

"Give it to me!" he demanded.

"We're not goblins," said Kirsty. "You can't order us around or scare us into doing what you say."

Jack Frost shook the last bits of fairy dust from his cloak and glowered at the girls.

"I'm going back to Rainspell Island," he said. "I was the winner of two of the Rainspell Games events. You pesky girls have taken back all Melissa's objects, and I want a medal!"

He disappeared with a loud crack of thunder. At once, the cloud vanished too, and the sun shone down on the Fairyland Games. Rachel and Kirsty flew down to Melissa, and Rachel pressed the stopwatch into their friend's hand.

Instantly, the fountains of fairy dust started to shoot upwards. The sky was filled with glittering fairy dust, and fairy stewards zoomed up to measure the height of the fountains.

"We have a winner!" one of the stewards called out. "Olympia's fountain is the highest, with fifteen different colours!"

The crowd burst into applause and Melissa flew back to her podium.

"Thanks to Rachel and Kirsty, we can begin the third stage knowing that Jack Frost has been defeated," she said, holding up the sparkling stopwatch. "Three cheers for our human friends!"

Rachel and Kirsty felt their cheeks growing hot as the fairies cheered for them. Smiling, Melissa continued her announcement.

"The third and final stage of the Fairyland Games is the flying competition," she said. "There are five magical balloons hovering in the air, and the competitors have to fly around each one, loop the loop, and then return to land on the finish line. They will be marked on technique, speed and agility. May the best fairy win!"

The balloons were red, yellow, green, blue and purple, and all eyes were fixed on them as the first competitor – Zoe the Skating Fairy – flew into the air. The

crowd oohed and ahhed as she twisted and spun around the balloons. Every move she made looked perfect. She was followed by Gemma the Gymnastics Fairy, who added amazingly fast flicks and kicks to her performance.

"It's going to be really hard to decide on the winner," Rachel whispered to Kirsty. "They all look brilliant to me!"

The girls cheered and clapped each competitor, delighted to be able to see such incredible flying skills. When everyone had competed, Melissa flew over to the king and queen to discuss the performances. Then she fluttered across to her podium.

"I am delighted to announce that the overall winner of this year's Fairyland Games is ... Gemma the Gymnastics Fairy!"

Melissa smiled as Gemma gasped in surprise. "Gemma, please approach the king and queen to receive your medal."

Flushing with excitement and pride, Gemma landed on the royal platform and curtseyed. There was a respectful silence as the queen rose and placed a gold medal around Gemma's neck. Then the crowd erupted into cheers, claps and whistles. Melissa flew over to join the girls, beaming from ear to ear.

"Everything has worked out perfectly," she said. "I'm so happy!"

"There's just one thing left to do," said Kirsty. "Jack Frost is hoping to get a medal for taking part in the Rainspell Games, even though he doesn't deserve one. We should probably go back to the

human world, in case he starts to cause trouble."

Melissa nodded and raised her wand.

The Real Winners

There was a bright, magical flash, and then the girls found themselves back on Rainspell Island, standing among the cheering crowd of spectators. Melissa tucked herself under a lock of Kirsty's hair.

"Look," said Rachel, gazing at a makeshift stage that had been set up on the beach. "They're about to announce the overall winner."

The competitors were standing beside the stage, and Kirsty nudged Rachel when she saw Jack Frost among them. His chest was puffed out and he kept darting triumphant looks at the other competitors.

"He looks very smug, doesn't he?" said Rachel. "Surely he won't be rewarded after all the cheating he did?"

"I don't know," said Kirsty, feeling anxious. "Perhaps he will be declared the winner because the Rainspell Games ended before we found the final missing object."

"Wait and see," Melissa whispered in her ear, a smile in her voice.

The chief organiser, Leo Read, stepped up to the microphone at the front of the stage.

"Welcome to the Rainspell Games award ceremony!" he declared. "We're

delighted that so many people came along today to support and encourage our competitors. It has been an exciting and dramatic event, with lots of last-minute twists and turns. Having reviewed all the events and exchanged notes with the stewards, I am delighted to announce that the winner of this year's Rainspell Games is … Ethan Hauxwell!"

Jack Frost's smug expression was wiped from his face. Rachel and Kirsty reached out and squeezed each other's hand.

"They've realised that he cheated during the events," Kirsty whispered. "Thank goodness."

"He must have been disqualified," said Rachel.

Glowering, Jack Frost elbowed his fellow competitors aside and stomped away from the beach.

"I never want to hear the word 'games' again!" he muttered.

No one except the girls noticed him go. The crowd was too busy cheering and applauding as a young man with brown hair stepped up to receive his medal. Melissa gave Kirsty a tiny kiss on the cheek, and blew a kiss to Rachel.

"Thank you for everything you did today," she said. "It's all because of you that the Rainspell and Fairyland Games were a success."

"It was our pleasure," Kirsty whispered.

Melissa vanished back to Fairyland with a shimmering sparkle, just as the girls' parents appeared.

"Wasn't that an exciting tournament?" Mrs Walker exclaimed.

"The competitors were incredible," Mr Tate agreed.

"They must be amazingly fit," said Mr Walker. "I'm astonished that *any* of them completed all three events! What about you, girls? Would you ever like to take part in the Rainspell Games?"

Rachel and Kirsty shook their heads and then grinned at each other.

"We've taken part in a game of our own today," said Rachel in a low voice. "It was called 'Help the Fairies'!"

"Yes," said Kirsty with a laugh. "And we had so much fun with our friends! When everyone plays fair, we're all winners!"

Now it's time for Kirsty and Rachel to help...

Esther
the Kindness Fairy

Read on for a sneak peek...

"It's so amazing to be back on Rainspell Island again – together!" said Kirsty Tate, leaning out of her window and taking a deep breath of sea air.

Her best friend, Rachel Walker, clapped her hands together and bounced up and down on her tiptoes.

"Today is the start of the most amazing summer holiday ever," she said. "I'm sure of it!"

They were sharing a room at the Sunny Days Bed & Breakfast, on the island where they had first met and become best friends. They were so happy to be on holiday together there again. The girls shared a quick hug before rushing down the narrow stairs to the cosy breakfast room. Their parents were already there, poring over leaflets about things to do on the island.

"I'm sure we can find some new things to do," said Mr Walker, "even though we have visited this island so many times before."

"How about a nice long hike?" suggested Mr Tate, as the girls slipped into their seats and poured out some cereal. "It'd be interesting to explore more of the island – we all love coming to see its beautiful plants and trees."

Rachel and Kirsty shared a smile. They had an extra-special secret reason why they loved Rainspell so much. It was here that they had first become friends with the fairies!

"Hiking would be a great start to the holiday," said Mr Walker. "Let's set off after breakfast, shall we?"

"Here's an interesting leaflet," said Mrs Walker, holding out a bright yellow flyer. "It's called the Summer Friends Club."

Rachel took the leaflet and read out loud. "'A play scheme for children staying on the island. Make new friends and join in lots of fun activities.' It sounds brilliant!"

As Kirsty and Rachel were looking at the leaflet and chattering about the activities, the breakfast-room door opened and Mr Holliday came in. He ran the bed and breakfast, and he glanced at the leaflet as he put some toast down on the table.

"My daughter Ginny's helping to run that club with her best friend Jen," he said.

Kirsty and Rachel exchanged a special smile, wondering if Ginny and Jen's friendship was as strong as theirs. They knew that they were lucky to have each other.

"Is it OK if we go to the Summer Friends Club instead of going on the hike?" Kirsty asked. "It sounds like lots of fun."

"Of course," said Mr Tate. "We'll see you later and hear all about it."

"The Summer Friends Club is meeting at Rainspell Park," said Mr Holliday. "I'm sure you'll have a wonderful time."

When they had finished breakfast, the Tates and the Walkers put on their rucksacks and walking boots and set out on their hike. Rachel and Kirsty waved goodbye and then headed off towards Rainspell Park.

Read **Esther the Kindness Fairy** to find out what adventures are in store for Kirsty and Rachel!

Join in the magic online by signing up to the Rainbow Magic fan club!

Meet the fairies, play games and get sneak peeks at the latest books!

There's fairy fun for everyone at

www.rainbowmagicbooks.co.uk

You'll find great activities, competitions, stories and fairy profiles, and also a special newsletter.

Find a fairy with your name!